I0530602

About the Book

Three friends—eleven adventures—one good time.

Before Flipper is kidnapped in front of Allison and Josh (details in the book Vetrix), the three best friends had a relatively normal life, though these short stories show that even ordinary kids doing everyday activities experience extraordinary moments. What kind of fun lies inside these pages?

- Josh and Allison get kicked out of a field trip
- They each share their most embarrassing moment
- Flipper uses his best pick-up lines on a girl he has a crush on
- The kids play a prank on Christmas night
- Allison and Flipper help Josh deal with a bully
- An indoor activity sends one of them to the emergency room
- Flipper and Allison battle against a tarantula that is stalking them
- Flipper fights a goat
- Allison becomes a sleuth
- … and more

Experience the trio's friendship as they have a good time together, no matter the circumstances.

About the Authors

Bill Bush grew up in Yates Center, Kansas, and is a graduate of Yates Center High School and Tabor College, where he earned a Master's degree in Accounting. He is a CPA and runner as well as a writer, is author of several collections of short stories, and has written a column in the Harvey County Independent since April, 2013.

His desire to write comes from his mom, Phyllis Roth Lewis, who was a published author and wrote numerous short stories, poems, and books.

Bill lives in Halstead, Kansas with his two teenage children, who are the inspiration behind many of his stories. You can learn more about Bill at www.billbushauthor.com.

Blake Bush is a fourteen year old eighth grader in Halstead, Kansas, who also takes three high school classes.

For several years he has attended Space Camp at the Cosmosphere in Hutchinson, Kansas. He loves video games and is a self-proclaimed Nintendo nerd. His next favorite activity is to annoy his older sister.

Blake is a member of the Halstead Middle School cross country, track, and Scholar's Bowl teams.

More information: www.snaderpublishing.com

Flipper, Allison, and Josh:

BEFORE VETRIX

Blake Bush and Bill Bush

Flipper, Allison, and Josh: Before Vetrix
published by Snader Publishing Company, Halstead, Kansas, USA
This book is also available as eBook.

First published 2017

© 2017, all rights remain with the authors
© 2018, cover design by Katharina Gerlach

printed On-Demand Publishing LLC, 100 Enterprise Way, Suite A200, Scotts Valley, CA 95066, USA, www.createspace.com

ISBN-13 978-1-945871-23-8

More information can be found on the publisher's website:
http://www.snaderpublishing.com

I want to thank Kaitlyne Page and Kaden Lopez for joining Blake Bush as the cover models of the first edition. My deepest appreciation goes out to you and your parents.

I also want to thank my cousin, Deb McLain, for making an awesome cover for the first edition and for doing it quickly.

TABLE OF CONTENTS

PROLOGUE

If you've read their story in the book, *Vetrix*, then you know all about Flipper, Allison, and Josh and the adventures that lie ahead for them. This short venture into their past will be a treat as you see how three of your favorite pre-teens enjoyed a normal life before that extraordinary Halloween night.

If you have not yet read *Vetrix*, then you are about to meet three best friends—Flipper, Allison, and Josh. You will get a glance into the friendship that knits them together. It's these bonds that will play an integral part in moving them each forward in *Vetrix*.

The following stories take place during their fifth and sixth grade years in school—BEFORE Halloween in sixth grade. The stories are not in chronological order. As you will soon learn, they live in Roswell, New Mexico, which may be a hint at the looming events of *Vetrix*.

For more information on Vetrix and other books by Bill and Blake Bush, please visit billbushauthor.com, or search their books on Amazon.

Thank you for your interest in Flipper, Allison, and Josh. We hope you enjoy their exploits.

SLEDDING INSIDE

Flipper loosely gripped the book in both hands. He moved his thumb and fingers back and forth causing the book to flip up and down. It was his trademark activity - where he got his nickname. It was a habit, probably a compulsion. He paced as he flipped, which meant he was deep in thought.

He was in his cousin Allison's upstairs bedroom with their best friend Josh. The three fifth graders had been playing video games, but Allison's mom told them to find something to do that didn't involve a screen. This meant, of course, they were now bored.

Josh jumped up from the floor. "I know! Let's slide down the stairs."

Two minutes later they were in the hallway looking down the steep staircase, almost drooling. Allison sat in a clear tote waiting to be launched.

Flipper was worried Allison might get hurt. "How is she going to stop?"

"She'll stop at the bottom." Josh stated like the answer was obvious.

"But what if she crashes?"

Flipper's question caused them to pause, each pondering the revealed risk that had previously escaped them.

They lined the walls with pillows and padded the bottom of the stairway with cushions and blankets. Flipper insisted on going first to make sure it was safe. He wore Allison's bike helmet, had on a pair of goggles instead of his normal black-rimmed eyeglasses, and was tightly secured in the tote he was sharing with three blankets.

Allison peered from the bottom of the stairway holding her IPad just below eye level, recording this historic feat.

"Are you ready?" Josh asked.

Flipper leaned forward. He stuck his left arm, his dominant, in the air giving Josh a thumb's up, then laid his arms on the sides of the tote.

"One, two, three." At three Josh pushed Flipper over the edge.

The next day Flipper would agree that sliding down the stairs in a tote was a bad idea, but for the first eight steps he was having as much fun as he did when he played video games. Unfortunately, the staircase consisted of thirteen steps.

On the ninth step the front of the tote caught and sent Flipper and the tote tumbling. It turned out the bike helmet was a good idea. Another good idea would have been arm pads. Flipper instinctively reached out to break his fall. It would be only seconds before he realized that was a terrible idea.

Flipper lay at the bottom of the stairs trying not to cry. The pain in his left arm and the large lump near his wrist made that extremely difficult.

Five hours later Flipper woke up in the hospital bed, his arm in a cast. The first face he saw was his mom.

She smiled and gently brushed his hair back from his forehead. "The surgery went well. You have to wear a cast for a few weeks but your arm is going to heal just fine."

Flipper's dad, his Aunt Lavon, Allison, and Josh were also in his hospital room.

"Did you get it recorded?" Flipper muttered.

Allison nodded her head but didn't speak.

"It was great!" Josh exclaimed. "It might have won money on America's Funniest Videos."

"What do you mean 'may have'?" Flipper asked.

Aunt Lavon put her arm around her daughter. "Allison erased the video. It was disturbing to watch." A tear fell from her eye. "I'm so sorry. I didn't know what you were doing. I would have stopped you..."

Flipper's dad cleared his throat. "Lavon, remember two years ago when Allison fell and broke her arm while I was watching them at the park?"

Lavon nodded her head.

Dennis smiled. "Well, I guess now we're even."

MYSTERY OF THE BASEBALL CARDS

Allison was stumped.

She had spent the summer reading her mom's old Nancy Drew books and was sure she could be a teenage sleuth - or in her case a sixth-grade pre-teen sleuth. She had solved several mysteries at school but this one had her baffled.

"So your baseball cards that we looked for all weekend showed back up this morning in your locker?"

"Sounds to me like you left them in your locker over the weekend and just forgot," Flipper interjected as he joined Josh and Allison in Josh's back yard. They sat on the meticulously cut grass in the shade of one of the two Arizona Ash trees for relief from the early September sun.

Flipper was Allison's cousin and Josh was their best friend.

"I know they were missing when I left school Friday afternoon," Josh stated emphatically.

Allison changed the subject and asked Flipper, "What took *you* so long?"

"I bumped into Neva. She lost her cell phone again."

"She's always losing stuff," Josh added.

It was true. So far Neva was Allison's most frequent client. "Last week I helped her find her cell phone three times."

"She could use your help again," Flipper suggested.

"Well, she's going to have to wait this time. I have a more challenging case."

"But it sounded to me like Josh has his baseball cards back?" Flipper asked confused.

Allison handed the box of cards to Flipper. She clumsily climbed into the hammock that stretched between the two shade trees. She placed her hands between her head and the pillow and stared absently into the overlapping branches. "That's the big mystery now. Why would someone take Josh's baseball cards then return them?"

Flipper shrugged his shoulders. "Maybe they felt bad and just wanted to give them back."

"Maybe..." Allison started to concede.

"But the cards are organized." Josh grabbed the box of cards from Flipper. He thumbed through them, pulled one out and handed it to Flipper. "And there's a new one. "This is Joe DiMaggio! I've never had a Joe DiMaggio card."

Flipper was doubtful. "Are you sure?"

"Trust me. I would know if I had a Joe DiMaggio card," Josh said defensively.

Flipper returned the card. "If you couldn't figure out who took them how are you going to find out who returned them?"

Allison scowled. She quickly rolled to her side to make sure Flipper had a good view of her angry eyes, but lost her balance as the hammock slid right out from underneath her. Josh and Flipper snickered, but she immediately stood and reasserted her glare, not wanting the boys to forget she was insulted.

"I would have solved the mystery *before* they were returned if I could have investigated the scene of the crime. We couldn't get into the school over the weekend so I wasn't able to search his locker. And I couldn't search his locker today because I went to my great aunt's funeral." She finally allowed herself to brush off the grass that stuck to her clothing when she fell, then declared, "Tomorrow morning we're going to school early to look for clues."

The next morning Josh turned the combination to his locker and it clicked. He beamed. "It only took me twice. I finally got the number memorized."

He opened the door and immediately bent down to pick up the two books and several loose sheets of paper that tumbled out.

"We've been in school less than a month and already your locker is a mess," Allison kidded.

"It's been that way since the first day," Flipper teased.

Josh held the books and paper that had tried to escape and stepped away from the locker so Allison could have a look. He didn't argue with their observation of his sloppiness.

Allison was hesitant. "You don't keep food in here, do you?" She was concerned about grabbing something moldy or gross.

Josh hesitated, which told Allison what the probable answer was. "I can't make any promises," he admitted.

As she sat on her knees she began removing things from his locker one item at a time, placing them neatly in a stack on the floor.

Suddenly she sprang to her feet and almost screamed with joy. She held her hands behind her and hopped up and down on her toes with excitement. "I've solved the case! In fact, I've solved both cases!"

Josh and Flipper looked at each other in bewilderment.

"Both cases?" Josh asked. "You mean who took the cards *and* who returned them?"

"No, no, that's just one case." Allison held out her hand so Josh and Flipper could see what she was holding. "The second case I'm talking about is where Neva lost her cell phone."

FLIPPER'S CRUSH

After school, Allison, her cousin Flipper, and their best friend Josh sat on Flipper's front porch and discussed the case Allison had solved that morning. Josh lay across the two-person glider with his head resting on the arm. Flipper held a stick he had picked up from his yard as he sat on the wood floor with his back against a post. Allison sat on a comfortably cushioned chair.

"Why do *you* think Neva took your baseball cards, organized them, added a Joe DiMaggio card, then gave them back to you?" Allison asked.

Josh shrugged. "I don't know."

Allison was astonished. "You haven't wondered why she did it?"

Josh shook his head. "My dad told me not to bother because I'd never be able to figure out why girls do things."

Flipper laughed and gave Josh a fist bump. Allison wanted to hit them both.

She almost pleaded for Josh to understand. "The only reason Neva organized your baseball cards is because she has a crush on you."

"She can't like *me* because Flip..."

"Dude!" Flipper cut him short.

Allison's jaw dropped. "You like Neva?"

Flipper remained steel-jawed and silent as his red cheeks spoke for him.

Josh continued like he had Flipper's approval to speak freely. "Of course he does. He's liked her since she sat next to him during the final assembly of school last year."

"Dude! Why are you telling her all of this?" Flipper was flabbergasted.

Josh sounded insulted. "It's your cousin Allison."

"I know who it is," Flipper retorted. "I told you not to tell anyone."

"I didn't know you meant Allison."

"Of course I meant Allison. She's a part of anyone."

Allison jumped in. "Well, I think it's sweet."

"See! That's why I didn't want you to tell her."

"It's not a big deal," Allison tried to console him.

"That's what I've been trying to tell him," Josh agreed.

"You should tell Neva you like her," Allison urged Flipper.

"No way!"

"Why not?" she asked.

"You said it yourself - she likes Josh."

"Oh." Allison paused, her enthusiasm suddenly deflated. "Oh yeah, that's right."

"But I don't like her," Josh said as if that made everything fine. "I've been telling Flipper for months to say something to her."

Allison looked at Flipper. "How does she act when you're with her?"

"He wouldn't know. He's been avoiding her," Josh answered for Flipper.

"What do you mean?" Allison asked. "He's been avoiding telling Neva he likes her?"

"He tries to avoid being around her, and he only talks to her when she speaks first." Josh explained.

Allison's mind was racing and she could feel her excitement rising again. "That's it, Flipper! You just need to spend time with her, let her get to know you better so she can see how great you are."

"Well, maybe..." Flipper began.

"Try one of your pickup lines on her," Josh suggested.

"Pickup lines?" Allison hesitantly inquired.

"He has some great ones!"

Flipper nodded his head in agreement. He stood and paced, flipping the stick up and down with both hands, a clear indication he was thinking. "Okay, I got it!" he exclaimed. He spread his arms wide and fluttered his eyebrows several times. "Well, here I am. What were your other two wishes?"

Allison hung her head and moaned. "We've got a lot of work to do."

FLIPPER AND NEVA

Flipper couldn't believe it. He was going to tell Neva he had a crush on her.

It had been four months; ever since she sat next to him at the school assembly at the end of fifth grade and her leg brushed against his. That was the moment he saw fireworks, that his heart sprang into his throat, that his stomach did a summersault. Before that moment he hadn't paid much attention to girls.

Since that moment he thought about 'the touch' - a lot. He thought about Neva even more. Her naturally tanned skin, her long, black hair, and the way she intertwined English and Spanish when she spoke too fast.

But it was more than the way she looked. She was fast - the fastest girl in the sixth grade. She was also smart and got good grades.

Flipper didn't know why she wasn't popular. Maybe it was because she was a little odd and quiet. That didn't matter to him because he thought those were good qualities.

For four months he kept his feelings secret from everyone except his best friend Josh, who had kept his secret until yesterday. Flipper was horrified when Josh told Flipper's cousin, Allison, that Flipper liked Neva. Once they both knew, it didn't take them long to talk Flipper into telling Neva he liked her. He had wanted to do it since the 'moment', but he had been too afraid.

He was still afraid, and not completely convinced he could actually go through with it. But he was determined. At least he was last night with Allison and Josh encouraging him. Now that he had slept, his courage was waning.

All the way to school he rehearsed the twenty-seven pick-up lines he had memorized the last few months in anticipation of approaching Neva. He still didn't know which one he wanted to use; there were so many good ones.

He didn't hear a word any of his teachers said all morning. He was too scared and nervous. After what seemed like three days, their lunch period arrived. He didn't even try to eat. He went outside where all the sixth graders hung out after lunch. He hoped to catch Neva alone so he could talk to her.

Flipper paced in the playground, alone. He found a short stick and picked it up. He flipped it up and down with both hands as he walked. His nerves continued to rise as he thought about Neva. What would she say? Would she laugh at him? Would she want to hang out with him? What if she liked him too? What if he couldn't go through with it?

"Flipper," Allison whispered adamantly. "Flipper, here she comes."

He looked up and saw the playground filled with sixth graders. He hadn't even noticed he was no longer alone. Neva was walking in his direction, not toward him but in his general direction. He looked at Allison, his eyes bulging as if shouting that he couldn't go through with it.

"You'll be fine." Allison gently nudged him in Neva's direction. "Just do it."

When he didn't budge, Allison shoved him hard enough he nearly ran into Neva. She stopped to avoid the collision. He had to say something to her now. "Hi Neva," he managed. "Sorry."

She smiled. "That's okay."

It was harder than doing chores, but he spit it out. "Would... would...would you grab my arm so I can tell my friends I've been touched by an angel?"

Neva giggled. "Oh, Flipper! You're so funny!" She put her hand on his arm, below the short sleeve so her hand was touching his skin. "Oh, there's Josh. I gotta go."

Flipper stood frozen like a statue. Neva was gone.

"I'm sorry, Flipper," Allison said in a soft, compassionate voice.

"Did you see that?" Flipper looked at his arm where Neva had held it. "She touched me! She touched my arm." He walked away starry-eyed.

FLIPPER'S PICK-UP LINES

"Are you sure about this?"

Flipper had used one of his best pick-up lines yesterday on his crush, Neva. He believed it went well - she had giggled and touched his arm - but Neva still liked Josh. Since Josh didn't feel the same way about Neva, Allison talked him into telling Neva so she could stop thinking about him, which might give Flipper a chance. At first Josh didn't want to talk to Neva, but Allison was persistent and he relented, mostly because Flipper was his best friend. She went with Josh for that conversation, and now she was going with Flipper to help him talk to Neva.

"I know it went well last time but I'm still scared." Flipper shook his arms nervously.

"Just be yourself," Allison said.

"What if I don't know what to say?" Flipper asked a little panicky.

"If you're stuck, just ask her a question. Everyone likes to talk about themselves. Here she comes."

Neva smiled. "Hi Allison. Hi Flipper."

"Hi Neva!" Allison elbowed Flipper when he didn't respond.

"Um, um, did it hurt?"

"What?" Neva asked, confused.

"When you fell out of heaven?"

Neva giggled.

Allison elbowed Flipper again. What was he thinking? When neither of them said anything for several seconds, Allison asked, "Are you going to the game tomorrow night?"

Neva nodded. "I want to if my dad will let me."

"Is your dad an alien?" Flipper chimed in.

There were a few moments of awkward silence.

Neva hesitantly said, "No. Why?"

Flipper quietly answered, "Because there's nothing else like you on Earth."

Neva giggled again and Allison swore she was blushing.

Flipper seemed to be gaining confidence. "Are you a magician?"

Neva smiled. She was hanging on Flipper's every word. "No, why?"

"Because every time I look at you everyone else disappears."

There was no doubt now, Neva's cheeks were red. Her giggles turned into laughter.

"Were your parents thieves?"

Neva shook her head.

"They must be because someone stole the stars from the sky and put them in your eyes. Do you have a map?"

Neva was laughing too hard to answer, which didn't slow Flipper down at all.

"I need one because I keep getting lost in your eyes."

Allison couldn't stand to watch any more. She loudly cleared her throat. "Flipper, can I see you a minute." She pulled on his arm and they walked several feet away from the hysterical Neva.

Allison whispered, "What are you doing?"

Flipper shrugged his shoulders. "You told me if I didn't know what to say to ask her questions."

"I meant ask her questions about her and what she's interested in. I didn't mean bombard her with lousy pick-up lines."

"Hey!" Flipper protested. "These are some of my best lines."

Allison sighed. "That's all you've said to her."

"I can't help it. I open my mouth to ask a question and the only thing that comes out are pick-up lines." Then Flipper grinned. "Well, she's getting to know the real me."

"I tell you what," Allison continued to whisper so Neva couldn't hear. "I'll start the topics and you follow my lead."

Flipper agreed.

They rejoined Neva.

Allison apologized. "Sorry about that. We were just talking about how we were looking forward to fall and the cooler weather."

That was his cue. Flipper searched for what to say. "Yeah, it's hot, Neva. You're hot. I mean, you're hotter than the bottom of my laptop."

Neva giggled so Flipper continued. "Did the sun come out or did you just smile at me?"

Neva melted. "Ahh!"

Allison shook her head in disbelief. She tried to change the subject again. "Do you go to church?"

Neva nodded. "I go with my parents to Grace Community Church."

Allison looked at him in anticipation. Flipper met her eyes. His eyes were watering. He realized he was holding his breath and exhaled deeply. Allison adamantly shook her head. She was going to kill him but he couldn't resist. "Somebody better call God because he's missing an angel."

He slowly walked around Neva without taking his eyes off of her. When he completed the circle he said, "Where do you hide your wings?"

He was positive she snorted when she laughed. He could feel Allison's ire, but he couldn't stop. He didn't know what else to say and his mouth just seemed to have taken over.

"What time do you have to be back to heaven?"

Neva laughed even harder.

"When God made you he was showing off."

Neva was laughing so hard her face was red and she wasn't breathing. She removed her glasses and wiped her eyes.

"Your eyes are blue like the ocean. And baby, I'm lost at sea!"

"Oh, good grief," he heard Allison mumble before she walked off.

After dinner that evening, he met Allison at Josh's house to talk about his encounter with Neva.

"How did it go?" Josh eagerly asked.

"It was horrible to watch."

"I tried to act normal, I really did! But every time I opened my mouth, one of my pick-up lines came out. It seemed like once I started I couldn't stop. That's all I could remember."

"It was that bad, huh?" Josh asked.

"Actually, she really thought it was cute," Flipper said. "In fact, she was flattered that I liked her."

"I hear a 'but' coming," Josh interjected.

"We agreed just to be friends."

"I'm sorry," Allison consoled. "Are you okay?"

Flipper smiled. "Actually, I'm relieved. It was a lot of pressure trying to impress Neva."

Josh shook his head. "Gosh, you worked so hard to memorize all of those pick-up lines. I thought surely one of them would work."

"Actually, one of them did."

Josh scrunched his head and Allison wore a puzzled look. "What do you mean?" she asked.

"Before we agreed to be just friends," Flipper explained. "She responded positively to my final pick-up line."

"Which one was that?" Josh asked.

Flipper's cheeks turned red. "Your lips look so lonely... Would they like to meet mine?"

EMBARRASSING MOMENTS

Josh double bounced on the diving board and dove into the pool. When he hit the water his swimsuit scooted down to his knees. He frantically pulled it up before he resurfaced.

He looked around expecting everyone to be laughing at him. He scanned the pool but no one paid him any attention. He couldn't believe his luck. "That was close," he said to himself, then swam to the four-foot area and joined his best friends, Flipper and Allison.

"I just had a horrible scare."

"What happened?" Allison asked, concerned.

"When I dove off the board, my shorts fell down. I barely got them pulled up."

Flipped laughed. "That would have been embarrassing!"

"It would have been awful!" Allison agreed.

"What's your most embarrassing moment?" Josh asked Flipper.

Flipper answered immediately. "It was in third grade P.E. I really had to go to the bathroom. We were doing sit-ups. When I finished, I noticed Melanie staring at me with her mouth open. I looked down and I had peed a little."

"You didn't notice?" Josh asked astonished.

"Not until I saw the wet spot on my shorts."

"What's yours?" Allison asked Josh.

"Last year we flew to California to visit my mom's family. On the flight home we sat in the second row from the front. I went to the bathroom in the back of the plane. As I walked back to my seat I noticed people were laughing. When I sat down, a guy in a seat across from me pointed down the aisle. I looked and saw a string of toilet paper from the bathroom all the way up the aisle. It had stuck to my shoe and I had drug it in front of everybody.

"Oh, that's horrible," Allison laughed.

"The worst part was walking back down the aisle to pick it all up."

"So what's your most embarrassing moment?" Flipper asked Allison.

Allison thought for a moment. "Last year in Mr. Burke's Social Studies class he asked a question and I blurted out the answer without even raising my hand."

Flipper gasped. "Did they suspend you?"

Allison giggled and splashed him. "Shut up. I wasn't finished. Anyway, he said 'Are you sure?'"

There were several moments of silence. Finally, Josh asked, "What happened?"

"That's it," Allison explained. "I got the answer wrong in front of everybody!"

Flipper continued mocking her. "I don't think I can hang out with you anymore."

"That's not a big deal. I get answers wrong all the time," Josh countered. "Besides, that's not your most embarrassing moment. Remember after the soccer game last spring we saw that boy you like - Alex. You saw him wave and you waved at him all excited but he was actually waving at his friends behind us and not you?"

Flipper laughed hard. "That's *so* embarrassing!"

"I DO NOT like Alex!"

"You do too," Josh argued. Then doing an imitation of her he said, "You turned red and waved like he was a movie star!"

Allison splashed Josh then jumped on his back and dunked him. Josh had an alarming sensation that was confirmed when he got his head above water.

"Is that brown in the water?" Flipper asked.

Josh was horrified. "I think I have a new most embarrassing moment."

THE TERROR OF THE TARANTULA

Flipper was beyond thrilled that Allison decided to hang out with him. He used the excuse that they needed to study for their science test the next day, but he could easily do that on his own. He just didn't want to spend the evening alone.

His parents were hanging out with friends from church and would be gone for several hours. Being a fifth-grader, Flipper had stayed home alone many times. Tonight was different though. It was dark before they left and it was almost Halloween. He had watched more than one scary movie that had him a little freaked out.

To make matters worse, Roswell was experiencing a rare thunderstorm. Lightning frequently flashed across the sky as the thunder boomed. He was nervous and was grateful for the company.

They sat at the dining room table with the screen door open a few inches. The cool breeze felt nice and Flipper liked the refreshing smell of the rain. The covered deck kept rain from coming in the house.

Flipper was a good student and got almost all As. Allison wasn't satisfied with regular As—she strove for perfection. They had studied for over an hour, and even though Flipper thought he was more than prepared for the test, he continued to study—or at least look like he was studying—because Allison wanted to.

Another thirty minutes passed. Flipper was bored. He began to wonder if it was worth having Allison over if she wasn't going to do anything fun.

She finally broke her silence. "I'm getting cold."

He was glad to have an excuse to get up. Flipper shut the door and went to the bathroom. He had just sat down at the table when a loud crash boomed outside and everything went dark.

Allison screamed and Flipper jumped, knocking his chair over backwards.

Panting heavily, he carefully felt his way into the kitchen. "Dad keeps some flashlights in the junk drawer" he told Allison.

A few moments later he had a flashlight in hand and gave one to Allison. He went to his room and called his parents on his mom's cell phone that she left for emergencies. She told him they were also without power and would get back home as soon as they could, but it was a twenty minute drive under good conditions. Flipper set the phone on his nightstand and returned to the kitchen.

"My parents are coming home but it's going to be a little while."

"Maybe I should call my parents to come over," Allison said nervously.

Flipper didn't want to admit he was scared but that did sound like a good idea.

Suddenly Allison screamed, threw her flashlight and jumped onto the top of the table.

"Why did you do that?" Flipper scolded.

He shined his light on her and she pointed. "There's a giant spider over there."

Flipper followed the direction of her finger with the light until it rested on a large, black tarantula. "Ahh!" he hollered and hopped up onto a chair.

More thunder cracked as Allison and Flipper both shook. He flippantly said, "Wouldn't our parents be proud of us now?"

Flipper climbed onto the table, careful to keep the flashlight shining on the tarantula.

"Turn it off," Allison demanded. "I don't want to see it any more."

The tarantula moved a few feet down the hallway.

"I'm not taking my eyes off of it. I want to know exactly where it is," he explained.

"Okay, that's a good idea," Allison conceded.

As if he was listening, the ugly beast scampered into Flipper's bedroom, filling him with a wave of horror.

Allison breathed laboriously. "I want to call my parents. Can I have your phone?"

"Sure," Flipper readily agreed. "Help yourself. It's on my nightstand."

She slapped his arm. "I'm not going in your room with that... that thing in there."

Flipper chuckled. They sat in silence for several minutes.

Another loud boom shook the house and made them both flinch.

The tarantula returned to the hallway and slowly walked halfway toward the table with Flipper and Allison's eyes glued on it.

"What are we going to do?" Allison said in a panic.

"We could kill it?" Flipper tentatively suggested.

"I'm not going near it!" Allison retorted.

Flipper wasn't about to either. "Hold this." He handed the flashlight to Allison and picked up his science book.

"What are you doing?" she asked.

He slid to the edge of the table. "I'm going to try to kill it." He carefully aimed and tossed the book like a frisbee toward the spider.

The light went straight toward the ceiling as Allison covered her eyes. Flipper peeled the flashlight from her fingers and shined it back on the spider.

The book lay between them and the hairy creature. "I missed."

He gave Allison the flashlight and took a second shot with Allison's science book. This time he threw it too far and the tarantula scurried until it was standing on top of the first book he had thrown.

Flashes of light continued to fill the room as the lightning show outside intensified.

They sat dejected for several minutes, resigned to their temporary prison and evil warden, who seemed content to stand guard from on top of the science book and mock them in horror.

"I have an idea." While Allison held the flashlight for him, Flipper stood on a chair and leaned against the wall. He supported his weight with one arm and slid the back door open with the other.

Next he hopped with the chair until he could crawl onto the counter that separated the dining room and kitchen. He gathered all of the silverware in a large bowl and returned to the table without touching the floor.

"What are you doing?" Allison asked inquisitively.

"The tarantula ran away from the books when I threw them. I'm going to see if I can chase him outside."

He tossed the silverware one utensil at a time toward the intruder. It wasn't long before the tarantula scurried away from the falling debris and escaped out the back door.

Still using a chair to avoid the floor, Flipper quickly shut the door and retreated back onto the table.

When Flipper's parents returned to their dark house forty-five minutes later, they encountered science books on the floor, utensils scattered throughout the hallway and dining room, and their son and niece sitting on the dining room table.

"What on earth happened in here?" Flipper's dad asked in astonishment.

"It was a lot like the movie Home Alone," Flipper explained. "Only scarier."

Herding Goats on the Farm

"Who wears crocs to the farm?"

Flipper grinned at his cousin Allison, who liked to tease him. "I'm not about to run around out here barefoot."

Allison rolled her eyes. She should have known better than to expect a serious answer from him.

Flipper, Allison, and Josh lived in town and weren't used to the farm. It was Mother's Day and Allison's parent's cousins—Flipper thought that made them third cousins but wasn't sure—had invited Flipper and Josh's families to join them for a cookout.

Allison stopped short. "Uh, oh."

"What is it?" Josh asked, concerned.

Flipper scanned the farm and didn't see anything worthy of an uh-oh.

She pointed toward an open gate. "That's the pen where the goats are kept."

They ran to the gate but the pen was empty.

"We need to get the goats back into the pen."

"How do we do that?" Flipper asked.

Before Allison could answer him, Josh shouted, "There's one!"

He ran to the goat and got down on all fours. Josh tried to convince the goat he was one of them but the goat wouldn't follow. Josh persisted as Flipper and Allison watched in amusement. When Josh said, "baa!" Flipper laughed so hard he fell to the ground.

"Goats don't baa, lamb's do!" Allison hollered.

"What sound do goats make?" Josh asked, still on his hands and knees.

Flipper was laughing too hard to answer, which was convenient since he didn't have any idea what sound a goat made.

"I don't know," Allison admitted.

While Josh continued to work on the goat, Allison and Flipper ran to the back porch. They selected items to help them herd the goats back to the pen; Flipper a plastic bat, Allison a broken broom handle, and for Josh, Flipper took a plastic gun.

Josh thought the plastic gun looked neat and finally abandoned his goat impersonation.

The items helped. They had two goats in the pen and almost had the third when one of the captured goats escaped.

When Flipper turned to go after the goat he felt something rub against his bottom. He startled and instinctively spun and whacked the brown goat with the plastic bat.

The goat let out a loud scream that sounded like a frightened child, then lowered its head to butt Flipper. In an attempt to get away, Flipper back peddled through the gate.

The goat followed Flipper into the pen, which was the good news. The bad news was that it seemed intent on getting even with Flipper for clobbering it in the head.

Flipper wanted to run but was afraid to turn his back on the angry goat. As he quickly stepped backwards he wildly swung the bat in front of him, occasionally bonking the goat on the head. In spite of this, the stubborn goat continued toward him.

He stepped in a mud puddle and his croc stuck. He frantically tried to pull his foot out of the mud. In his panic, Flipper jerked his leg up, lost his balance, and fell over backwards. As he scrambled to get up before the goat ate him alive, he swung hard and nailed the goat one last time. Then Flipper left his croc in the mud and bolted for the fence. He hopped up and climbed over the fence, narrowly escaping the charging goat.

"I thought you didn't want to run around the farm barefoot?" Allison chuckled.

This time it was Josh who collapsed on the ground laughing.

FIELD TRIP TO THE UFO MUSEUM

Allison bounced up and down on the bus seat.

"Stop it!" Josh barked. "I almost spilled my drink."

"It has a lid."

"That doesn't mean it can't spill."

"You two have been bickering all morning," Flipper complained from the seat across from them.

They were on a field trip to the UFO Museum. Allison had lived in Roswell, New Mexico—home of the supposed 1947 alien crash—all of her life, yet had never been to the museum.

In fact, she hadn't realized how much she wanted to go until her teacher announced the trip two weeks ago on the first day of sixth grade.

Unfortunately, her cousin Flipper and their best friend Josh didn't want to go. She wasn't about to let them keep her from enjoying the experience.

When they arrived, all the kids set their drinks on an empty table, away from the main area. There were dozens of displays with pictures and articles. Allison made a beeline to the closest display. She wanted to read them all! Before she got started her teachers called everyone together and introduced the tour guide for the morning.

"Welcome to the Roswell UFO Museum. We are open from nine to five, seven days a week. I'm going to walk you through the museum and tell you about the crash of 1947. Please feel free to ask any questions along the way. Follow me to the first exhibit."

"This is crazy," Josh complained.

"And boring," Flipper added.

Allison scolded them. "Shh! This is interesting."

"Disney princess fairytales are more interesting...and realistic." Josh gave a wry smile.

"You have no taste," Allison spat.

Flipper stepped between them. "You two are getting on my nerves."

For thirty minutes the tour guide led them through the museum, explaining the events that occurred on July 2, 1947, and talked about other UFO sightings. Allison hung on every word. She loved space and hoped there were really aliens out there somewhere.

When the tour ended, they got a ten-minute bathroom break. Allison, Josh, and Flipper got their drinks. Josh sucked on his straw and spit it all over his arm. Allison and Flipper laughed.

"Why did you do that?" Flipper asked.

"This is awful!" Josh lifted his lid and exposed a ketchup packet on the end of his straw.

Allison laughed, thinking that justice was done. Josh had been a pain all morning and had it coming to him.

Josh glared at her. "Why did you do that?"

She gasped. "I didn't do it!"

"Right!" Josh said with thick sarcasm.

"Josh, clean that up immediately," their teacher, Mrs. Smith, ordered.

"I'll get you back," Josh muttered to Allison.

***

Josh and his family had moved to Roswell three years ago. He still hadn't gotten used to all of the signs of aliens around the town. A flying saucer on the front of the Wal-Mart building? He thought it looked ridiculous.

He didn't understand why it was such a big deal, but a big deal it must be. Here he was with twenty-one of his classmates suffering through the UFO Museum. Josh was bored, irritated with Allison, and couldn't get the taste of ketchup from his mouth. He had no use for this field trip.

The longer their tour guide droned on and on about aliens, the more Josh had become determined to prove the alien crash false. He didn't think anything could redeem the trip—until the alien showed up.

The tour guide wore an alien costume; Josh loved costumes and found himself listening intently as the tour guide/alien explained what it was like to come from another planet to Earth. As an alien, the tour guide even had a sense of humor.

"I want one," Josh declared to Allison and Flipper when the alien departed.

"Want what?" Flipper asked.

"The alien costume."

"I should have known you would like that."

"I thought you didn't like aliens," Allison said snidely.

"I didn't say I did," Josh mimicked her tone.

Allison lifted the straw to her lips and stopped. She removed the lid and peered inside. After a close examination she decided it was safe and tipped her cup and drank.

Not only did Josh and Flipper laugh, but so did several other students around them. Allison stopped drinking and watched the laughing kids suspiciously. The laughter ceased but everyone continued to stare her direction. When Allison lifted the drink toward her mouth again the laughter returned.

She glared at Josh and he shrugged his shoulders, smiling mischievously. One of their classmates pointed to her cup. Allison cautiously tilted the cup. Written across the bottom in large, black letters was the word DUNCE.

"Josh! I swear!"

"Allison! Josh! Come here!" Mrs. Smith barked.

They glared at each other but obeyed. Mrs. Smith marched them out the back door. "I want you two to wait outside while the rest of the class has snacks. Whatever is going on between you two, work it out. The bickering ends now." She stormed back into the museum.

Josh noticed a metal door leading underground and took a seat on it, his chin in his hands. "I love cookies." He said dejectedly.

Allison sat beside him. "They're playing a game where you have to answer questions about the museum and it's history. I know I would have won."

Josh chuckled. "Who could beat you?"

"Josh, I'm sorry I laughed at you."

"But you're not sorry you put ketchup in my soda?" Josh's gaze remained forward.

"I didn't do it," Allison insisted. "Besides, you humiliated me by writing on the bottom of my cup."

"I didn't do it." Josh sighed.

Josh's eyes grew wide. He spun toward Allison and their eyes met. At the same time they shouted, "Flipper!"

* * *

Flipper sighed contentedly. He didn't have to listen to Josh and Allison bicker any longer. With no one looking, he tossed the extra ketchup packet in the trash and replaced the sharpie in the pencil holder beside the cash register.

Flipper shoved a cookie into his mouth—his third—and smiled satisfactorily.

Halloween Party

If Josh had his way every day would be Halloween. He loved to dress up—not in the sense of wearing nice clothes, but by imitating other characters or people. Some years he wore two or three different costumes on Halloween. It just wasn't fair he had to contain his costume wearing to one day a year.

This year was different; he wore the same outfit all day long—an old Pittsburg Pirates jersey with the number 21 on the front. Although Pittsburg was not his favorite team (that was the Tampa Bay Rays), baseball was his favorite sport and Roberto Clemente was his favorite player of all time. Josh's grandparents were from Puerto Rico, just like Clemente. Josh knew all his stats—3,000 career hits, 4 batting titles, 12 gold gloves, and a .317 lifetime batting average.

At school, most of his fifth grade classmates didn't know baseball history so he explained over and over and over again who Roberto Clemente was. He was thrilled to do so. He was proud of his heritage and astonished to learn that most of his class didn't know Puerto Rico was a territory of the United States. He worried that he bored them with information, but he couldn't help himself. Once he got started his enthusiasm and love for baseball and Puerto Rico took over.

Most of the kids patiently tolerated Josh's excited ramblings. One student, a sixth grader, made fun of him during lunch and put him down for being nerdy. The bully gave Josh such a verbal chastising that he lost his enthusiasm. The rest of the day Josh was unusually quiet. Even when his friends tried to encourage him to talk about his costume by asking questions Josh mindlessly quoted facts. He couldn't pull himself out of his funk.

That evening Josh's dad dropped him and his best friends, Flipper and Allison, off at the church. Neither Flipper nor Allison had a sibling but they were cousins and were often mistaken for brother and sister. So this year they decided to dress up like Princess Leia and Luke Skywalker. They both dressed in white. Allison's mom fashioned her long, red hair so she had two buns, one on each side. Flipper wore a karate robe and carried a lightsaber.

The party was fun—games, snacks, and a costume contest—but the highlight was the haunted house. Josh, Allison, and Flipper were one of the last groups to go through. Josh didn't admit it but he was nervous. As much as he liked Halloween he didn't like ghosts and witches and being scared. Flipper and Allison knew this about him but no one else did. He did what anyone his age would—he pretended to be excited about the haunted house and went through.

Allison and Flipper were the kind of friends that wouldn't make fun of him when he screamed. In fact, Allison took his hand half way through. This helped a lot. He was disappointed when she let go just before they entered the last room. The last room was always the scariest. That's when he needed her the most.

As they stepped through the door Josh had to shield his eyes to protect them from the burst of light. When his eyes adjusted he was astonished at what he saw. Twenty-seven fifth graders wearing Roberto Clemente Pittsburgh Pirates jerseys.

CHRISTMAS NIGHT PRANK

Josh missed his parents.

His dad was deployed overseas and his mom had gone to visit him. This wasn't the first time both of his parents had been overseas without Josh, but it was the first time it had happened at Christmas time.

He thought it would be no big deal. He was twelve, after all. Besides, he got to stay with his best friend, Flipper, and his family. He had fun at first, but now that Christmas Eve had arrived, Josh was miserable.

Allison and her parents joined them for dinner. Also visiting was Flipper's great-aunt who had Alzheimer's and kept asking the same questions over and over again.

He didn't mind that so much. She was nice and kept giving him pieces of candy—more than he could possibly eat. But she never laughed or smiled. She seemed, tense, and anxious and miserable.

Josh worried he would hurt her feelings or excite her too much. His parents had lectured him about being on his best behavior, which meant no practical jokes. That was like torture for Josh! So far his parents would be proud of him, but he felt like he wasn't able to be himself.

Since Allison was Flipper's cousin, her parents agreed to let her spend the night with Flipper and Josh. They settled in Flipper's room—Flipper and Josh in his queen-sized bed and Allison on the floor.

With the house quiet and dark Josh felt lonely. He tried not to think about how much he missed his parents by talking to Flipper and Allison well into the night. In fact, they chatted so long that Josh' dinner wore off.

"I'm hungry."

"Now I am too," Flipper said.

"There's some summer sausage in the fridge," Allison suggested.

The three fifth-graders tip-toed down the stairs as quietly as they could. As they went through the living room they saw that the meager selection of presents under the Christmas tree had grown substantially—Santa had visited!

After a substantial snack they snuck into the living room to snoop.

Josh saw his name on a small present about the size of the video game he hoped to get. He felt another pang of loneliness. He knew his parents had left gifts for him to open, but it wouldn't be the same without them.

His need to be ornery and his need to get his mind off of his parents collided.

"What do you say we have a little fun?"

"What do you have in mind?" Allison asked.

"Let's move everything around." Josh didn't think they would go for such a large task at—he looked up at the large, decorative clock—one forty-one in the morning, but they agreed.

Allison took a picture of the tree and presents with her phone. They moved the couch away from the wall and placed the presents on it. Flipper crawled underneath the seven-foot artificial tree. Josh pulled on the high branches, Allison the low branches, and Flipper pushed against the tree stand. Slowly, they inched their way across the carpet.

When they made it to the other corner, Flipper said, "We only knocked off five ornaments. Not bad."

They pushed the recliner to where the tree had been, the love seat to where the recliner had been, then the couch to where the loveseat had been. Allison pulled up the picture of the tree and presents on her phone and they intentionally placed the presents back under the tree.

"Quiet!" Allison whispered with sudden urgency.

The two boys froze. They listened and remained completely still for an agonizingly long five minutes. A toilet flushed; a door opened; footsteps down the hallway, then a bedroom door closed.

Flipper let out a deep breath. "That was my great-aunt."

"That was close," Josh added.

They got back to work. After a long and painfully tedious process of matching the presents to the picture—which Flipper and Josh didn't think was near as important as Allison did—the three beamed with pride. Flipper and Allison collapsed onto the couch while Josh ran to the restroom. What he saw in there gave him another idea.

"We need to wish everyone a Merry Christmas," Josh said returning from the bathroom.

"How?" Flipper asked.

Josh smiled and held up a roll of toilet paper.

"How does toilet paper say 'Merry Christmas'?" Allison asked.

"We'll need some tape."

"I hate to ask," Allison said hesitantly while Flipper retrieved a roll of tape.

Josh brought a chair from the dining room to stand on and hung toilet paper from the ceiling so it drooped down in front of the tree, spelling out 'MERRY X-MAS'.

Finally, around three, the kids settled back into bed and fell asleep.

A few short hours later they awoke with a start at the sound of a scream. They rushed downstairs with Flipper's parents behind them.

Flipper's mom gasped.

"What happened?" Flipper's dad asked.

The sun shined brightly into the room, illuminating the tree. Even with toilet paper hanging from the ceiling and the room's furnishings rotated ninety degrees, everyone's attention was elsewhere.

At the bottom of the stairs, Flipper's great-aunt stood, laughing hysterically.

Vetrix: Chapter 1

Flipper was a normal twelve-year-old kid, or so he thought. Little did he know that a war several million light years away between the Gudes and the Snaders was about to change his destiny. Then again, the Gudes and Snaders didn't realize Flipper was about to change theirs either.

***

"It's Friday *and* Halloween." Allison, who was dressed up as Athena, lamented. She wore a long flowing toga and a crown on her head. She loved reading about the Greek gods, and her favorite author was Rick Riordan. Allison had even named her dog Anna, after Annabeth in the Percy Jackson books. She continued, "I don't think teachers should be allowed to assign major projects when they know everyone's going to be squirrelly. I mean, the school encouraged us to dress up and they still expect us to be able to concentrate in class?"

Flipper sat next to Allison in Social Studies thumbing through his notecards before the bell rang. He was dressed as a Nerd. His short-sleeve, button-up shirt was partially untucked and he had a pocket protector and pens in the front pocket. His jeans were pulled up way too high. Flipper wondered how anyone actually wore them like that all the time. He had tape around the middle of his glasses and his normally straight, blond hair was black, greasy, and combed with a center parting. He had come to school with a sign on his back that said *Kick Me*, but a teacher made him take it off when everyone kept doing just that.

"Allison, you're in sixth grade now. It's time to grow up. Try to be more like your older, more mature cousin." Flipper patted his chest as if Allison didn't know who he was talking about. "Calm, cool and collected."

She rolled her eyes. "Good grief! You're eleven months older than me."

"Yes, but a person matures a lot in eleven months. You'll see."

Allison chuckled. Flipper could always make her laugh, even when she was stressing at school. She changed the subject. "Do you have your presentation ready?"

"Yes, but I can hardly think about it. I'm too excited about going to Carlsbad Caverns tomorrow."

They lived in Roswell, New Mexico, only an hour and a half away from Carlsbad, yet Flipper had never been there. He recently did a report on bats for school so his parents had promised they would take him to see the caverns. People sat outside the caves every evening to watch as the bats flew out, just over their heads. Flipper couldn't think of anything that sounded more exciting.

"Too excited?" Allison asked sarcastically. "What happened to calm, cool and collected?"

Flipper gave an uneasy smile.

"Hey, guys!" Josh said, coming into the classroom. Josh loved to dress up which made Halloween his favorite time of year. He was wearing an alien costume that had over-sized feet. His seat was right in front of Allison. Josh was tall for a sixth grader and his bulky costume made it difficult for him to slide into his seat, which was connected to the desk.

Allison and Flipper both giggled. They knew Josh didn't mind them laughing at him. He liked to be silly and make people laugh. Josh was thirteen but still in the sixth grade. His dad was in the military and when he was in the first grade they moved three times. He had to repeat first grade, which meant he was older than most of the students. He was also bigger, which gave him an advantage when playing sports.

"Okay, class," Mrs. Smith said, standing up from her desk. "It's time for our presentations. Josh, you're up first."

Getting up turned out to be harder than sitting down. Everyone in the class laughed at Josh's struggle to stand. Flipper was sure Josh was smiling, though no one could see it underneath the papier mâché alien head he wore.

Eventually, Josh made it to the front of the class and gave his report in a muffled voice. "My report is on the Roswell Incident. On the evening of July second, nineteen forty-seven, several people said they saw a disc-shaped object flying through the air. This was during a thunderstorm. The next day a local rancher outside of Roswell, New Mexico, claimed to have found a piece of what he said looked like an exploded aircraft. On July eighth, the Roswell Daily Record reported that the Air Force base in Roswell had captured a flying saucer. Although the Air Force claims that the flying saucer was simply an experimental weather balloon for a top secret project, many people today believe the United States military found a UFO spacecraft, captured the aliens, and covered up the truth.

"Now, every year, Roswell celebrates a UFO Festival during the first week in July. People from all over the world come to visit the museums, talk about aliens, and tour the crash site. My parents told me about the festival in nineteen ninety-seven, which was the fiftieth anniversary of the crash. Hotel rooms were sold out as far away as Albuquerque and Lubbock, Texas. Several celebrities, including Oprah Winfrey, were here. The theater at the mall had a pre-release showing of *Men In Black* and Will Smith was there signing autographs.

"I don't believe the crash was a UFO with aliens. That doesn't make any sense to me. It was storming and people wouldn't have been able to tell what they really saw. Besides, there is no real evidence to prove it was aliens. But, I think the city of Roswell is smart to promote the festival and for businesses like McDonald's and Wal-Mart to put aliens on their buildings. It helps them make a lot of money. The end."

Some of the kids clapped quietly.

"Thank you, Josh," Mrs. Smith said.

"Good job!" Allison and Flipper both told Josh, patting him on the shoulder as he sat down.

***

As Allison walked between Flipper and Josh after school, her waist-length bright red hair bouncing behind her, she looked at Josh, who was still wearing his alien head. "You know, Josh, I believe the crash in nineteen forty-seven really was an alien spaceship."

Although it was still a couple of hours away from sun set, the dark clouds gave the afternoon a dusk sort of feeling.

"Really?" Josh said with surprise.

"Yeah. There is so much we don't know, both in outer space and here on earth. My parents told me the government keeps a lot of secrets from us. Who knows, maybe there are aliens living here in Roswell." She shrugged her shoulders.

"I think Principal Hermann is an alien," Flipper's serious tone made it hard to tell when he was joking. "Have you seen the way she walks around all hunched-back? And she never smiles. If I was an alien from another planet, I wouldn't ever smile."

Josh shook his head. "My dad's been all over with the Air Force. He told me there was no way the military could be hiding aliens without him knowing."

"Maybe some people are good at keeping secrets," Allison said, dismissing Josh's argument. "What do you think, Flipper?"

He pushed his glasses up. "I don't know. It doesn't seem very likely. I mean, to keep a secret like that for this long. I think someone would have said something. But maybe, if…" Flipper stopped speaking as Allison stiffened and tightly grabbed his arm. Josh kept walking; with the alien head still on he didn't notice they had stopped.

Allison was staring across the street. Flipper followed her gaze. She seemed to be looking at the empty lot. In the back corner stood an evergreen—the kind that looked like a large Christmas tree—looking a bit out of place in the barren field. He saw sparse patches of tall weeds, lots of dirt, and a tumbleweed blowing across in the light, steady wind. He didn't see anything worth looking at, let alone to be frightened by.

He looked back at Allison. Her eyes were glued to the lot and the vein in her neck was bulging. He could tell she was scared but didn't know why. He suddenly felt cold and uncomfortable.

"Are you okay, Allison?" His voice betrayed his nervousness.

Other than her quick breaths and heaving chest, she didn't move or speak. Flipper's arm was throbbing from Allison's tight grip, but he did his best to ignore it. He felt desperate to help his cousin. "What is it? I don't see anything."

"I-I-I… I don't know," she finally stuttered. She blinked rapidly like she was coming out of a trance. Her eyes remained directed across the street and her speech was labored. "I didn't see anything either, but I could feel something. It was like a strong presence, like someone was across the street watching us."

Flipper looked again. "I still don't see anything."

Allison took a deep breath and relaxed. She let go of his arm, looking down as she did so. "I'm so sorry, Flipper!" He was bleeding where her nail-bitten, jagged fingernails had dug into his skin.

"Holy cow, Allison!" Josh walked back toward them. He removed one of his alien gloves and gave it to Flipper. "Here, use this to wipe the blood."

"I don't want to mess up your costume." Flipper tried to hand the glove back to Josh.

Josh waved his hand in refusal and said enthusiastically, "Putting blood on it will make it that much cooler."

Flipper hesitated, then held the glove over the cuts. "Thanks."

"What was that all about?" Josh asked, concerned.

"Allison thought she saw something," Flipper said with skepticism.

"Actually, I thought I kind of sensed something," Allison tried to explain again. "I had a strong feeling that someone was watching us—the most intense feeling I've ever had." She glanced back at the now obviously empty lot. "I don't know. I guess it sounds crazy. Maybe it is crazy."

"Maybe it was an alien," Josh said, raising his hands and walking towards her—more like a zombie than an alien.

"Stop it," she said, playfully pushing him away. Allison laughed as they began walking again. "But maybe it was an alien and only I can sense it because only I believe."

"Sports teams send scouts to watch players they might want to recruit," Josh said with rising enthusiasm. "Maybe you're being recruited."

Flipper laughed so hard he had to stop walking. "Does that mean she's an alien?"

Josh laughed with Flipper while Allison stood with her hands on her hips, visibly irritated.

"Remember, if I'm an alien, *you're* an alien. We're related."

Flipper stopped laughing. Josh laughed even harder.

***

"Flipper, is that you?"

Flipper, Josh and Allison had just come into the house after trick-or-treating later that evening. "Yes, Mom."

Flipper's mom hurried into the room. She was full of life and loved the holidays, but this was the first year she had let Flipper go trick-or-treating by himself. She had given them very specific instructions about where they could go, what they could do, and when they had to be back. They each carried a cell phone. But still, his mom worried. "How did it go?"

"It was okay," Flipper said without enthusiasm.

"Yeah, I think we are outgrowing the whole trick-or-treating thing," Allison said, slumping onto the couch.

"But not the candy," Josh said, dumping his sack onto the floor, eager to go through it.

"I'm just glad you're home safely," Flipper's mom said. "And not too much candy. I agreed that Josh and Allison could spend the night since they are going to Carlsbad Caverns with us tomorrow, but you promised you wouldn't stay up late."

"Yes, Mom." Flipper and Allison dumped their sacks on the floor and began eating and trading candy.

Two hours later Flipper, Josh and Allison were in their sleeping bags on the living room floor. Although they were only a few feet apart they could barely see each other. The burnt out streetlight left only the dim moonlight shining through the large front window to see by.

Flipper was giddy about their trip the next day and talked about it non-stop until Josh fell asleep and began to mumble about playing basketball and being stuck in quicksand.

Flipper went quiet and then looked at Allison. "Do you really believe there might be people on other planets? Or were you only teasing Josh?"

"I don't know. It's hard to look up at the sky and not think there are more people out there somewhere." Allison paused before deciding to continue. "But mostly I sense there are others out there. Sometimes I sense they are close—in Roswell. I haven't really talked about it because it sounds crazy. I know we were joking about it earlier, but sometimes I do wonder if I'm not from another planet."

Flipper laughed. "That would explain a lot."

Allison laughed too. "Yeah, I pretty much walked into that one."

Flipper smiled at her. "Good night, Allison."

"Good night, Flipper."

***

Allison's dreams that night were intense, and she didn't feel like she was dreaming. She felt like she had gone back in time—was reliving the previous day—but there was something quite different about this repeated experience, like a long déjà vu.

She was back in Social Studies class and Josh was giving his presentation on the Roswell Incident. Everything looked the same as it had that morning, but this time she was overwhelmed by the same strange sensation she had felt when walking home. She felt like she was in the presence of someone important; kind of like when she met the mayor at a dinner she went to with her parents. Except this felt like she was in the presence of someone much more important than a mayor.

Allison turned and looked behind her. In what had been an empty seat in the back row that morning sat someone she had never seen before. He was older than the students and had a slightly amused expression. His hair was rumpled and his skin was... She blinked, hoping her eyes would clear. His skin was... Allison gaped at him until he noticed her stare and looked her way. She jerked her head back to Josh, droning on about the Roswell Incident.

She felt the presence ease, so she looked back. The man was gone, but she couldn't get his image out of her mind.

His skin had been purple. Brightly, unapologetically purple.

Instantly, she was with Flipper and Josh, walking home from school. She froze sensing the same overwhelming presence as earlier. But this time, when she looked across the street at the lot, she saw the purple man from the classroom standing, watching them.

This time, she locked eyes with him for several moments. The purple man tilted his head, looking at her, puzzled. The look of confusion on his face mirrored what Allison felt. She looked at Flipper and saw her hand clamped on his arm. She looked back across the street but the man was gone.

Allison tossed and turned as her dream intensified.

She began having flashbacks to their evening of trick-or-treating. Everywhere they went, the purple man was there, watching, following. The sense of his presence intensified with each sighting. Finally, she couldn't take it any longer and started running towards him. She didn't know who he was or what he wanted, but she couldn't stand the feeling any longer. She was scared and angry. She screamed, "Just leave me alone!"

Allison startled awake and sat straight up, sweating, breathing heavily. She was awake, but the intense presence she had felt in her dream was still with her. In fact, it was even stronger. She jumped to her feet and turned around. The purple man was standing in the room with them, holding Flipper in his arms. Flipper was still asleep.

"What are you doing?" Allison demanded.

"We are trying to protect you. Blake… Flipper… has been chosen to save us all."

And with those words the man and Flipper vanished.

Two alien species. One threat to Earth.
But who is the real threat and who can be trusted?

Twelve-year-old Flipper didn't believe in aliens — until he was kidnapped by one.

When he wakes up one morning on the planet Vetrix he is trapped in the midst of an inter-planetary war. As Flipper struggles to survive and find a way back to Earth he discovers he may be a descendent of one of the warring species and that his intervening in the war may be his destiny, if destiny is decided by a computer program.

On Earth, Allison begins having dreams that turn out to be real experiences. When she watches a purple man disappear with her cousin, Flipper, no one believes her. Allison's best friend Josh agrees to help and together the two sixth-graders begin their own investigation that leads them to the truth behind the Roswell Incident of 1947 and current alien activity on Earth.

As they try to figure out how to expose the secret colony of aliens and their plans to destroy the human race, Allison attempts to use her dreams to locate and rescue Flipper.

Vetrix is the first book in the Flipper series.

available in print and as eBook

ISBN 978-1-945871-22-1

The battle for Vetrix is over. The battle for Earth begins.
Who can Flipper count on if not even his parents believe him?

After having returned safely from his adventures on the Gude home planet, Flipper is dismayed to find only ridicule and skepticism back home. Of course aliens aren't real; of course these are just the flights of fancy of a sixth-grader and his friends. Nobody believes his story. Nobody cares.

But when the Snaders put into motion a nefarious plot to conquer Earth and eliminate the human threat in one fell swoop, Flipper finds his story verified in a most spectacular—and horrifying—fashion. Not only have they sent a deadly fleet to attack Earth, but they have infiltrated the halls of power, insinuated themselves into the heart of human civilization … and now the trap is closing.

With the help of Josh and Allison, along with allies both old and new, Flipper will need to dig deep and find the courage to stand up against the Snaders once more, and prevent them from destroying everything he holds dear—friends, family, and the world itself.

Earth is the second book in the Vetrix series.

available in print and as eBook
ISBN 978-1-945871-21-4

Earth has just been saved. A secret weapon awaits the defeated Snaders.
Who can stop the rise of the deadliest threat the universe has ever seen?

With Earth secure for now and Flipper and his family safely holed away in the mountains, it seems that the worst of the Snader-Gude war is over. Allison still needs to be rescued, of course, but the Gudes will handle that on their own. There seems to be nothing more for Flipper and his friends to do, even if Josh is frustrated.

But when the two friends are kidnapped by aliens—again!—and taken to the mysterious planet Zentron, Flipper finds that the universe needs him once more to foil the ultimate Snader plot to activate a secret weapon, stashed away for the day of reckoning.

Aided by ever-faithful Josh and by Anna, Allison's dog, Flipper will have to do everything in his power to help the hapless Nerds of Zentron repel the coming Snader incursion and prevent the enemy from retrieving their most prized asset and gaining the power to turn the tide of the war on Earth.

Zentron is the third book in the Flipper series.

available in print and as eBook
ISBN 978-1-945871-19-1